FOLKTALES FROM AFRICA:

THE BABOONS WHO WENT
THIS WAY AND THAT

Also by Alexander McCall Smith

FOLKTALES FROM AFRICA:

The Baboons Who Went This Way And That

ALEXANDER McCALL SMITH

CANONGATE

Edinburgh · New York · Melbourne

This edition first published in 2006 by
Canongate Books Ltd, 14 High Street,
Edinburgh, EH1 1TE

1

The following stories first published in
The Baboons Who Went This Way And That in 2006
'Chicken, Hawk and the Missing Needle'
'Morategi and His Two Wives'
'The Miracle Tree'
'The Goat and the Jackal'
Copyright © Alexander McCall Smith, 2006

The following stories first published in *The Girl Who Married a Lion* in 2004
'Bad Uncles'
'The Grandmother Who Was Kind To A Smelly Girl'
'The Thathano Moratho Tree'
Copyright © Alexander McCall Smith, 2004

Other stories first published in *Children of Wax* in 1989 by Canongate Books Ltd

Copyright © Alexander McCall Smith, 1989

Illustrations copyright © Naomi Holwill, 2006

British Library Cataloguing-in-Publication Data
A catalogue record for this book is available on
request from the British Library

Typesetting and layout by Sharon McTeir,
Creative Publishing Services, Oldhamstocks, Dunbar, Scotland

Printed and bound in Great Britain by
Clays Ltd, St Ives plc

1 84195 772 0 (10-digit ISBN)
978 1 84195 772 2 (13-digit ISBN)

www.canongate.net

For Finola O'Sullivan

CONTENTS

Introduction

These stories are rather different. They are not stories which one person has written – they are stories which have been handed down from old people to young people over many, many years. Nobody knows who first told them; all we know is that they have been told for a very long time indeed.

The stories in this book are all from two countries in Africa – Zimbabwe and Botswana. I collected some of them by talking to people and asking them to tell me the stories – others were collected by other people who did the asking for me. Then I retold them in my own words, adding some descriptions to make the stories a little bit more vivid for those readers who do not know what Africa is like.

It is not easy to forget these stories – they remain in the mind for a long time after we have come to their end. Why is this? I think that it is because they seem so strange to us when we first encounter them. They are about animals who can talk. They are about very peculiar things that happen. In the real world a hawk would not be a friend of a hen, and in the real world trees do not suddenly change into something quite different. But all this happens in these stories.

They are not just stories of magical events, though. Folktales are often meant to say something about how we should behave towards other people, and you will see that message in many of these stories. They show that selfish people will be caught out sooner or later. They show that we must help those around us. They also warn us to beware of tricksters.

When you have finished reading these stories, I hope that you may have found out something about Africa. Modern Africa, of course, is not like the Africa in these stories, but many of the traditions of the past still remain – and many of the songs and stories too. The stories might help you to understand at least some of that traditional African culture.

Most of all, though, the stories are meant to be fun, and that, I hope, is what people will have when they read them.

Alexander McCall Smith
Edinburgh 2006

THE TALES

I

Guinea Fowl Child

A rich man like Mzizi, who had many cattle, would normally be expected to have many children. Unhappily, his wife, Pitipiti, was unable to produce children. She consulted many people about this, but although she spent much on charms and medicines that would bring children, she remained barren.

Pitipiti loved her husband and it made her sad to see his affection for her vanishing as he waited for the birth of children. Eventually, when it was clear that she was not a woman for bearing a child, Pitipiti's husband married another wife. Now he lived in the big kraal with his new young wife and Pitipiti heard much laughter coming from the new wife's hut. Soon there was a first child, and then another.

Pitipiti went to take gifts to the children, but she was rebuffed by the new wife.

"For so many years Mzizi wasted his time with you," the new wife mocked. "Now in just a short time I have given him children. We do not want your gifts."

She looked for signs in her husband's eyes of the love that he used to show for her, but all she saw was the pride that he felt on being the father of children. It was as if she no longer existed for him. Her heart cold within her, Pitipiti made her way back to her lonely hut and wept. What was there left for her to live for now – her husband would not have her and her brothers were far away. She would have to continue living by herself and she wondered whether she would be able to bear such loneliness.

Some months later, Pitipiti was ploughing her fields when she heard a cackling noise coming from some bushes nearby. Halting the oxen, she crept over to the bushes and peered into them. There, hiding in the shade, was a guinea fowl. The guinea fowl saw her and cackled again.

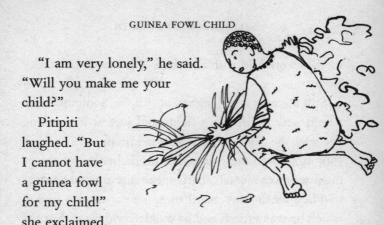

"I am very lonely," he said. "Will you make me your child?"

Pitipiti laughed. "But I cannot have a guinea fowl for my child!" she exclaimed. "Everyone would laugh at me."

The guinea fowl seemed rather taken aback by this reply, but he did not give up.

"Will you make me your child just at night?" he asked. "In the mornings I can leave your hut very early and nobody will know."

Pitipiti thought about this. Certainly this would be possible: if the guinea fowl was out of the hut by the time the sun rose, then nobody need know that she had adopted it. And it would be good, she thought, to have a child, even if it was really a guinea fowl.

"Very well," she said, after a few moments' reflection. "You can be my child."

The guinea fowl was delighted and that evening, shortly after the sun had gone down, he came to Pitipiti's hut. She welcomed him and made him an evening meal, just as any

5

mother would do with her child. They were both very happy.

Still the new wife laughed at Pitipiti. Sometimes she would pass by Pitipiti's fields and jeer at her, asking her why she grew crops if she had no mouths to feed. Pitipiti ignored these jibes, but inside her every one of them was like a small sharp spear that cuts and cuts.

The guinea fowl heard these taunts from a tree in which he was sitting, and he cackled with rage. For the new wife, though, these sounds were just the sound of a bird in a tree.

"Mother," the guinea fowl asked that night. "Why do you bear the insults of that other woman?"

Pitipiti could think of no reply to this. In truth there was little that she could do. If she tried to chase away the new wife, then her husband would be angry with her and might send her away altogether. There was nothing she could do.

The bird, however, thought differently. He was not going to have his mother insulted in this way and the

following day he rose early and
flew to the highest tree that
overlooked the fields of the new
wife. There, as the sun rose, he
called out a guinea fowl song:

Come friends, there is grain to eat!
Come and eat all this woman's grain!

It did not take long for the new wife to realize what was
happening. Shouting with anger, she ran out into the
fields and killed Pitipiti's guinea fowl and his friends.
Then she took them back to her hut, plucked out their
feathers, and began to cook them.

Mzizi was called to the feast and together he and his
new wife ate all the guinea fowl at one sitting. It was a
tasty meal and they were both very pleased with them-

7

selves for having made such a good start to the day.

No sooner had they finished the last morsel than Mzizi and the new wife heard the sound of singing coming from their stomachs. It was the guinea fowls singing their guinea fowl songs. This, of course, frightened the couple and they immediately seized long knives and stabbed at their stomachs to stop the noise. As the knives pierced their skins, bright blood flowed freely and they fell to the ground. As they fell, from out of the wounds came the guinea fowl and his friends, cackling with joy at their freedom. Soon they were back in the field, eating the last of the grain that was left.

Pitipiti was pleased that she no longer had to suffer the taunts of the new wife. She now owned her husband's cattle and because of this there were many men waiting to marry her.

8

All of them, of course, were happy at the thought that they might marry a wife who had such a clever and unusual child.

2

A Girl Who Lived In A Cave

A girl who only had one brother liked the place where she and her parents lived. There was a river nearby, where she could draw water, and the family's cattle enjoyed the sweet grass which grew by the riverside. The huts were shaded from the hot sun by the broad leaves of the trees, and at night there was a soft breeze from the hills, which kept them cool. Passers-by, who called in to drink water from the family's calabashes, would say how much they envied that quiet place, and how their own places were so much drier and dustier.

Then a terrible thing happened, which spoiled the happiness of the family. The girl had gone to fetch water from the river and was walking back to her hut with a large calabash on her head. Suddenly she began to feel that she was being followed. At first she did nothing, but then, when the feeling became quite strong, she turned round and looked behind her. There was nothing to be seen, although the tall grass moved and there was a faint sound, rather like that which a creature makes when it scurries through a bush.

The girl continued on her way. After she had taken a few more steps she again heard a noise. This time she swung round more sharply, dropping the calabash to the ground. There was a man behind her, crouching down, half in the grass, half out of it.

The girl was frightened by the sight of the man, but she tried not to show her fear. He smiled at her, and rose to his feet.

"You must not be afraid of me," he said. "I am just walking in the grass."

The girl could not understand why a man should

wish to walk in the grass, but she did not say anything. The man came up to her and reached out to touch her.

"You are a nice, fat girl," he said.

The girl was now very nervous and moved away from the man's touch.

"My father's place is just there," she said. "I can see the smoke from his fire."

The man looked in the direction of the huts.

"If that is so," he said, "I can walk with you to your father's place, where I can eat some food."

The girl walked ahead of the man and soon they came to the circle of huts under the trees. There the stranger waited at the gate while the girl went in to tell her father that there was a man who wished to eat some food. The father came out, called to the man, and invited him to sit on a stone under one of the trees. Food was made by the girl's mother and given to the man. He took it, and put it all into his mouth in one piece. Then he swallowed, and all the food was gone. The girl had not seen a man eat in this way before and wondered why he should be so hungry.

After the man had eaten, he got up and said goodbye to the father. He looked around him before he left, as if he was trying to remember what the family looked like and what they owned. Then he walked off and was soon obscured by the tall grass that grew in that part.

The girl went to stand by her father's side.

"That was a very wicked man," said the father. "I am very sorry that he visited this place."

"I am sure he will not come back," the girl said. "He was going somewhere else when I met him."

The father shook his head sadly.

"Now that he is here," he said. "We shall have to leave. I shall tell your brother to collect his sleeping mat and get ready for us to go to some other place."

The girl could not believe that the family would be leaving the place where they had lived for so long and of which she felt so fond. She tried to persuade her father to stay, but he was convinced that they were in great danger by staying where they were.

"It is better to move now," he said, "than to regret it later."

The girl wept, but her tears were ignored by her father. Soon he had all the family's possessions loaded on his back and was calling out to the others to follow him on the path.

"I shall not come with you," the girl said defiantly. "I have been happy in this place and see no reason to move."

The girl's mother pleaded with her to go, but the girl refused. Eventually the father became impatient.

"If you must stay," he said, "then you should at least go and live in a cave in the hillside. There is a place there where there is a large rock which can be used as a door. At night you must roll that rock in behind you and let nobody into the cave."

The girl agreed to this, as she knew that nearby cave. It was comfortable and cool, and she thought she would be happy there. As the rest of the family disappeared down the path that led to their new place, she took her mat and her pots to the cave and set them on a ledge at the back. Then, since it was beginning to get dark, she rolled the rock in the front into position. Inside the cave, it was pitch black, but the girl felt safe and she slept well that first night.

The next day, the girl's brother paid her a visit to see how she was. She told him of how comfortable she had been in the cave and of how well she had slept.

"I am safe there," she explained. "The rock blocks the mouth of the cave and I shall open it to nobody. If you come, though, you should sing this song and I shall know that it is you."

The girl then sang a short song, which the boy listened to. He kept the words in his mind, as he planned to visit the girl that night to make sure that she was safe and that the rock was acting as a strong enough door.

That evening, when he returned, it was already dark. As he approached the cave, he sang the song which she had taught him:

There is a rock here and the cave is dark;
Open the cave, my sister, and let me in.

When the girl heard this song, she knew straight away that her brother was outside. She pushed at the rock and it rolled to one side. Her brother was pleased to see that the song worked and that his sister was safe. He gave her the food that he had brought her and then said goodbye.

"Make sure that you roll the rock back once I am outside," he said.

"I shall always remember that," his sister replied. "A girl could not live alone in a cave like this unless she had a rock for protection."

The brother came the next day, and the day after that. On his third visit there was something that worried him. Not far from the cave he noticed that there were footprints on the ground and that lying nearby there was a bone which had been gnawed. He picked up the bone and looked at it. Whoever had eaten it must have had a great appetite, for his teeth had cut right into the

17

bone to extract its goodness. The footprints were large, too, and the sight of them made the brother feel uneasy.

He arrived at the front of the cave and began to sing his song. As he did so, he had a strange feeling – as if there was somebody watching him. He turned round, but all that he saw was the wind moving through the dry brown grass and a rain bird circling in the sky. He finished the song, and the girl rolled back the rock to let him into the cave.

"I would like you to come and live with your family again," he said to the girl. "We are sad that you are not with us."

"I am sorry too," she replied. "And yet I love this place too much to leave it. Perhaps one day my father will decide to come back here."

The boy shook his head. He knew that his father would never come back now that he had found that he liked the other place to which he had gone. Soon the memory of this place would fade and the family would talk no more about it.

The boy ate some food with his sister and then left.

As he walked away, he again felt that there was somebody watching him, but again he saw nothing but the wind and a small snake that moved like a dark arrow through the dry leaves on the ground.

The man who had driven the family away from that place was a cannibal. Now he had heard the boy singing his special song to his sister in the cave and he had remembered the words. Under a large tree not far away, he practiced the song which the boy sang. His voice, though, was too rough, and he realized that no girl would be fooled into believing that it was the voice of her young brother.

The cannibal had a way to deal with this. He made a fire, and on the fire he put a number of stones. Then, when these stones were red hot, he put them in his mouth and let them lie against that part of his throat that made the sound. After a few minutes he spat out the stones and tried the song again. The stones had done what he had hoped they would do and his voice was now as soft as the boy's.

Inside the cave, the girl had settled herself to sleep on her sleeping mat when she heard her brother singing outside. It surprised her that he should come back so soon, but then she remembered that he had left a calabash in the cave and might be returning to collect it.

"I am coming, my brother," the girl sang out. "The rock will move back and let you in."

By the time that the mouth of the cave was half open, the girl realized that it was not her brother who was standing outside. When she saw the cannibal, her heart gave a leap of fear and she struggled to roll the rock back. The cannibal, though, was too quick and had seized her before she could seal off the cave mouth.

The girl screamed as the cannibal lifted her off the ground and began to tie her arms and legs with a rope he had with him. Then, when she was firmly tied up, he went to a place nearby and began to make a fire so that he could cook the girl and eat her. As he made the fire, he sang a special song, of the sort that cannibals sing, in which he told of how a poor hungry cannibal had found a fat girl in a cave.

The girl wept with sorrow at the thought of what had happened to her. She wept for her father and mother, whom she would never see again, and she wept for her stupidity in trying to stay in so dangerous a place. Through her tears, she sang a sad song, about how a girl who lived in a cave was captured by a wicked cannibal.

The boy had felt so uneasy on his way home that he had come back to the cave. Now he was hiding in the grass, listening to the sad song of his sister. When he saw the cannibal bending over his fire, the boy rushed forward and pushed him into the flames. The many skins which the cannibal was wearing soon caught fire and he ran wildly away, letting out strange cries as he ran.

The boy untied his sister and then led her back to their father's new place. That night, the girl told her father of what had happened. He was worried at the thought of the narrow escape that she had had, but he was relieved that she was now safe. He was glad, too, to hear that the cannibal had run away, as this meant that the family could now return to that place where they had been so happy, and where the girl knew they would be happy once again.

3
Pumpkin

A family who lived near a river had good fields. Because they were near the river, there was never any shortage of water, even when other parts of the country were dry and dusty. There was no father in this family — he had gone off to a town and had never come back — and so the mother lived with her five sons and with her own mother and father. Although she sometimes wished that her husband would return, she knew that this would never happen, and so she reminded herself of her good fortune in having such good fields and such brave sons to look after her.

This family ate nothing but pumpkins. From the time when they had first come to that place, they had known that the ground was good for pumpkins. If you planted pumpkin seeds there, in a few months there would be large plants growing across the ground and, a few months after that, there would be great yellow pumpkins ripening in the sun. These pumpkins tasted very good. Their flesh was firm and sweet and would fill even the hungriest stomach. As the boys grew up, the woman saw that pumpkin was undoubtedly the best sort of food for a boy, as her sons were strong and took great pleasure in helping their mother in the fields.

Soon this family was known throughout that part of the country for their good pumpkins. People would walk from a great distance to buy spare pumpkins, and later they would tell their friends just how delicious these pumpkins were. The family planted more pumpkins, and soon they had so many in their fields that they were able to sell almost half of their crop, while keeping the rest for themselves.

One morning, the youngest boy, Sipho, went from the huts to fetch water at the river to water the pumpkins. He did not get as far as the river, though, as what he saw in the fields made him turn straight back. Calling out to his mother, he ran up to her hut and told her what he had seen.

The woman lost no time in running down to the fields. When she reached the first of the fences she let out a wail of sorrow.

"Our pumpkins!" she sobbed. "Who has eaten our pumpkins?"

The other boys and the grandfather were soon in the fields as well. They looked about them and saw that many of the pumpkins had been ripped from their vines and were lying, half-eaten, on the ground. Other pumpkins had been crushed, and the seeds were scattered all over the ground. Every field looked as if it had been a battleground, with the yellow blood of the pumpkins on every stone.

The whole family set to work in clearing up the broken pumpkins. Then, when this was done, they set to repairing the fences which had been broken by whomever had done the damage. That night, the two elder boys crouched in a bush near the furthest field, waiting to see if anything would come back to wreak further havoc.

Many hours passed, but at last they heard a sound. They knew immediately what it was that had done so much damage to their crop. Of course, they were too frightened to move, and had to sit in their bush while the great elephants ate as many pumpkins as they could manage and destroyed many more. Then, when the elephants had walked away, the two boys ran to their home and told their weeping mother what they had seen.

The next day the family discussed what could be done to save their remaining pumpkins.

"There is nothing we can do," said the grandfather, who was very old and had seen many times the damage that elephants could do. "When elephants come to a place the only thing that people can do is to move somewhere else."

"But we cannot leave this place," said the mother. "We cannot leave our beautiful fields and the good water in the river."

"Then we shall all starve," said the grandfather. "The elephants will eat all our pumpkins and there shall be none left for us."

Nobody spoke for a while. They all knew that what the grandfather had said was probably true. Then the oldest boy stood up.

"I know of a way to save our pumpkins," he said. "It is the only way."

The other boys looked at him as he spoke. This boy always had the best ideas, but they wondered how even he could deal with such great beasts as elephants.

"We shall put a boy in a pumpkin," he said. "We shall hollow out the biggest pumpkin that we can find and we shall put a small boy inside. Then, when the elephants come back to the fields, they will be unable to resist such a good-looking pumpkin. The biggest elephant will eat it, and when the boy is inside the elephant's stomach he can strike at its heart with his knife. That will surely drive the elephants away."

Everybody agreed that this was the best plan that could be suggested.

"You will have to get inside

the pumpkin," the oldest boy said to his youngest brother. "You are the smallest."

The small boy was unhappy about this plan, but since the whole family had agreed on it, he could not refuse to play his part. While the older boys went off to the fields to look for the biggest pumpkin, the mother made a special meal for her youngest son. Then she covered him with fat and gave him some special charms that she had kept for such a time.

The other boys came back to the house with the largest pumpkin that the family had seen that year. They set it on a low rock and cut a hole in its side. Then, with wooden scoops and knives, they took out the pumpkin flesh and put it in a cooking pot. Soon the pumpkin was quite hollow and they were able to push the youngest boy inside it.

It was now getting dark, and so they carried the great pumpkin down to one of the fields and placed it in the middle. No elephant could fail to spot such a delicious-looking pumpkin.

Do not be afraid," they said to their young brother. "There is nothing that can go wrong with this plan."

Inside the pumpkin, the small boy stayed quite still. If he moved, he thought it possible that an elephant would become suspicious. He had a long time to wait, and it was cramped inside the pumpkin, but, like all his brothers, this boy was brave.

Some hours passed before he heard the first sounds of the elephants. To begin with there was only a faint rumble, and then the whole earth seemed to shake as the

31

elephants entered the field. The largest of the elephants, who was also their leader, looked about the field as he wondered which pumpkin to eat first. When he saw the big pumpkin in the middle, he knew immediately that that would be the best pumpkin to eat. He went across to it, sniffed at it briefly with his trunk, and then scooped it up into the air and straight into his mouth.

Inside the pumpkin, it seemed to the boy as if the whole world was turning upside down. He felt the hot breath of the elephant as the trunk embraced his pumpkin and then he sensed the sides of the pumpkin squeezing as the vegetable passed down into the great creature's throat. When the movement stopped, he realized that he was now inside the elephant's stomach. This was the time for him to cut his way out of the pumpkin and find the elephant's heart.

His knife in his hand, the boy groped his way out of the pumpkin. With a quick lunge, he struck his knife into the heart of the elephant, and then fell to his knees as the great beast roared out and lurched upon his feet.

By the time that the family arrived, the other elephants had all run away in fright. Alone in the middle of the pumpkin field, the great elephant lay on his side. The boys cut through the thick elephant skin to rescue their small brother. The mother kissed him when he emerged from within the elephant, and then she wiped away the fat and the pieces of pumpkin that stuck to his skin.

The following night, many people came to see that family to help them eat the elephant meat. They ate many pumpkins too.

4
Milk Bird

A man who had two clever children — a boy and a girl — used to go to a place where he knew there were succulent wild fruits to be picked. This man knew a great deal about fruits, and he was always able to distinguish between those which were good to eat and those which were bitter in the mouth. His family, who all liked these fruits, used to wait to meet him in the evening and enjoy the food which he brought back from that special place.

It was while the man was gathering fruits that he saw a most unusual bird. There were many birds in the fruit place, as they liked to eat the seeds which the fruits produced. Many of the birds in that part were bloated from the goodness of their food, and could not fly as high or as quickly as other birds. For this reason, if anybody wanted to catch a bird, then that was the easiest place for it to be done.

The unusual bird was standing in the grass, his head barely showing. If the man had not been looking in that direction, he would have missed him, but, as it happened, his eyes alighted on the bird's head and he drew in his breath in astonishment.

On the top of the bird's head there was a plume of feathers. These feathers were not grey, as were the feathers on top of the snake-eating birds, but were coloured red and green. The neck, which could just be made out, was white.

The man watched the bird, which had not seen him and was showing no sign of fear. After a moment or two, the bird strutted forward a few paces, and so the man was able to see more of its body. He saw now that the belly was covered with red feathers and those on the bird's long legs were white and black. The bird moved its head, as if looking for something, and took a few more steps.

The man watched the bird for a few moments. There was a great deal of fruit that had ripened that day, but he found that he could think only of the bird and of how he would like to take the bird home. He was worried that if he approached the bird, it would take to the air and disappear, but he knew that if he did nothing he would never be able to forget

that he had lost the chance of capturing the
most beautiful of all birds.

The man crept forward, taking care
not to allow his footsteps to be heard.
There were twigs on the ground, and large
stones, but he avoided these carefully and
was soon only a short distance away from
his quarry. Then, with a great lunge, he flung
himself on top of the bird and pinned it to the
ground.

To the man's surprise, the bird did not struggle.
As it lay beneath him, its wings and its body immo-
bile, it merely looked up at him with its dark eyes, and
blinked.

The man took out his fruit bag and slipped the bird
into it. Then, deciding not to bother to gather any
more fruit, he turned round and made for
home as quickly as he could. He could not
wait to see the surprise of his children when
they saw the marvellous bird which he had
found.

When he arrived home, it was almost dark and the
children had gone into their huts. The man sat at
his wife's side and told her of the bird he had
found.

"It is a most unusual bird," he explained.

"There are many people who would like to have a bird like this one."

The woman asked him to open his bag, and he did so, making sure that the bird was unable to fly out of the open neck of the bag. The woman looked in and let out a cry of surprise.

"I have heard of that sort of bird before," she said. "That is the sort of bird which gives milk."

The man was most surprised that his wife should have heard of so unusual a bird, but he knew that her father had been a man who knew the names of all the birds and that she must have obtained her knowledge from him. Carefully reaching into the bag, he took the bird out and held it before his wife. She quickly fetched a calabash and began to milk the bird. After only a few moments, the calabash was full with sweet-smelling milk, which the man and the woman both drank. Then they put the bird into a spare hut which they had and closed the door.

The next morning the woman went into the hut and, after waiting a few moments for her eyes to become accustomed to the darkness, she sought out the bird and milked it again. Then she took the calabash of milk to her children, who drank it all and asked for more.

"You may have more tonight," she said. "From now on, there will always be such milk for you."

*   *   *

The children were delighted with the fresh supply of such delicious milk. Every morning they drank their fill, and their parents finished off the rest. With all the milk they were getting, the children began to grow larger and sleeker, and their skin shone with good health.

At the end of a month, the children began to be inquisitive about the source of the milk.

"I don't understand how we get such sweet milk from our cows," the girl said to her mother. "They have never given such milk before."

The woman smiled, and said nothing.

"Perhaps you have a secret cow somewhere," suggested the boy.

Once again the mother said nothing. She did not

want to tell her children that what they were drinking was bird's milk, as she had heard from her father that children did not like to think they were drinking milk from birds. If they stopped drinking the milk, then they would surely lose all the fat which they had put on and which made them so much admired by everybody else in that place.

The girl went to her brother that evening and said that she had a plan. The next day, they would put a small bowl of the milk outside and wait to see which animals came to drink it. In this way they would know where the milk came from and their curiosity would be satisfied.

When their mother gave them the calabash the next day, the girl poured a little of the milk into a bowl and gave it to her brother. He slipped out of the hut and put the bowl down at the edge of the bush. Then the two of them watched, waiting for the first animal to drink the milk.

A hyena walked past, sniffed at the milk, but did not drink it. Then there came a baboon, who peered into the bowl, but did not touch the milk. The baboon was followed by a rock rabbit, which also showed no sign of wanting to drink the milk. At long last, a bird landed near the bowl, and soon had his beak dipped in the milk. After him there came more birds, until the bowl could not be seen for the fluttering of wings about it.

"That is bird's milk we have been drinking," the boy said. "Now we know."

The children were keen to see the bird from which their parents were obtaining the milk, and so they hid in a place where they could watch their mother as she came out of her hut in the morning. They both saw her go to the empty hut and look about her before she opened the door. Then they saw her come out again with the calabash in her hand and they knew immediately that the bird was being kept in that hut.

"We shall go and see the bird when our parents are in the fields," the boy said. "I have heard that birds which give milk are very colourful."

That afternoon, as the man and the woman were in the fields, the two children crept up to the bird's hut and opened the door. Once inside, they looked about nervously and it was a few minutes before they saw the bird sitting in his corner. The bird watched them suspiciously. He had grown used to the man and his wife, but the children were unfamiliar.

The children approached the bird and looked closely

at him, while the bird stared back with its dark eyes, and blinked.

The boy looked at the bird's feathers and shook his head.

"It is sad," he said. "The bird has lost all the colour from his feathers."

When it heard this, the bird looked down at his own feathers and sighed.

"It is because I have been kept in here for so long," the bird said to the boy. "I have not seen the sun for many weeks."

The boy shook his head.

"I am sorry," he said.

"If that is so," said the bird, "you should take me out into the sunshine for a few minutes. A short time in the open air would restore all the colours to my feathers."

The boy and the girl agreed to do this for the bird. Carefully they lifted him in their arms and took him out into the open. Then they set him down on a low branch of a tree and watched the colour return to his feathers. It happened quite quickly, and soon the bird was no longer faded.

"He is looking happier," the girl whispered to her brother. "His feathers are normal again."

"Thank you," said the bird. And with that, he flew up into the air and had soon disappeared. The girl looked at the boy and wailed.

"We shall never be forgiven," she said. "We shall never find a bird like that again."

The boy was frightened of telling his father what had happened, and so he went out into the hills to look for another bird which was exactly the same as the bird which had escaped. He searched in all the places he knew birds liked, but in none of these did he find a bird which looked at all similar. On his way home, though, he was surprised by a strange sound in the grass. There, sheltering behind a small bush, was a bird which looked almost the same as the milk bird. The boy seized the bird, which did not resist but just looked at him, and blinked.

That night the woman went to milk the bird in its special hut. After she had finished, she brought the calabash out and gave it to her husband. He raised it to his lips and took a sip.

"This is not milk," he said. "It is water. Why has our bird given us only water?"

The woman was unable to answer his question. She

went back to the bird and tried again to milk it, but once more all that the bird gave was water. This made the woman wail, as she could think of no reason why the bird should suddenly have turned against them in this way.

The next day, while their parents sat under a tree and mourned the change in their bird, the two children crept out into the bush to see if they could find another bird that would give milk. They felt responsible for the loss of the first bird, and they knew that sooner or later they would have to confess to their parents what had really happened. They walked far, and eventually they came to a place where there was a group of boys calling out in excitement. They ran over to join the group of boys and saw that they had surrounded a bird and were throwing stones at it and calling it names.

The boy and his sister were angered at the cruelty of the boys. They seized two large sticks which were nearby and drove the other boys away, telling them that it was wrong to surround such a bird and torment it. Then they looked at the bird, which was lying on the ground, its breast trembling with fear. At once they knew it was the milk bird.

Gently, the boy lifted up the milk bird and carried it home. Without being seen by the parents, he took the bird into the hut and exchanged it for the water bird. The water bird then flew away, cackling with pleasure at its freedom.

The milk bird did not attempt to escape again. It was grateful to the boy and his sister and from that time on gave milk which was sweeter than ever before. The milk bird stayed alive until the boy and his sister grew up and left that place. Then it fell to the floor of its dark hut, its heart broken with sorrow.

5
Children
Of Wax

Not far from the hills of the Matopos there lived a family whose children were made out of wax. The mother and the father in this family were exactly the same as everyone else, but for some reason their children had turned out to be made of wax. At first this caused them great sorrow, and they wondered who had put such a spell on them, but later they became quite accustomed to this state of affairs and grew to love their children dearly.

It was easy for the parents to love the wax children. While other children might fight among themselves or forget to do their duty, the wax children were always dutiful and never fought with one another. They were also hard workers, one wax child being able to do the work of at least two ordinary children.

The only real problem which the wax children gave was that people had to avoid making fires too close to them, and of course they also had to work only at night. If they worked during the day,

47

when the sun was hot, wax children would melt.

To keep them out of the sun, their father made the wax children a dark hut that had no windows. During the day no rays of the sun could penetrate into the gloom of this hut, and so the wax children were quite safe. Then, when the sun had gone down, the children would come out of their dark hut and begin their work. They tended the crops and watched over the cattle, just as ordinary children did during the daytime.

There was one wax child, Ngwabi, who used to talk about what it was like during the day.

"We can never know what the world is like," he said to his brothers and sisters. "When we come out of our hut everything is quite dark and we see so little."

Ngwabi's brothers and sisters knew that what he said was right, but they accepted they would never know what the world looked like. There were other things that they had which the other children did not have, and they contented themselves with these. They knew, for instance, that other children felt pain: wax children never experienced pain, and for this they were grateful.

But poor Ngwabi still longed to see the world. In his dreams he saw the hills in the distance and watched the clouds that brought rain. He saw paths that led this way and that through the bush, and he longed to be able to follow them. But that was something that a wax child could never do, as it was far too dangerous to follow such paths in the night-time.

As he grew older, this desire of Ngwabi's to see what the world was really like when the sun was up grew stronger and stronger. At last he was unable to contain it any more and he ran out of the hut one day when the sun was riding high in the sky and all about there was light and more light. The other children screamed, and some of them tried to grab at him as he left the hut, but they failed to stop their brother and he was gone.

Of course he could not last long in such heat. The sun burned down on Ngwabi and before he had taken more than a few steps he felt all the strength drain from his limbs. Crying out to his brothers and sisters, he fell to the ground and was soon nothing more than a pool of wax in the dust. Inside the hut, afraid to leave its darkness, the other wax children wept for their melted brother.

When night came, the children left their hut and went to the spot where Ngwabi had fallen. Picking up the wax, they went to a special place they knew and there Ngwabi's eldest sister made the wax into a bird. It was a bird with great wings and for feathers they put a covering of leaves from the trees that grew there. These leaves would protect the wax from the sun so that it would not melt when it became day.

After they had finished their task, they told their parents what had happened. The man and woman wept, and each of them kissed the wax model of a bird. Then they set it upon a rock that stood before the wax children's hut.

The wax children did not work that night. At dawn they were all in their hut, peering through a small crack that there was in the wall. As the light came up over the hills, it made the wax bird seem pink with fire. Then, as the sun itself rose over the fields, the great bird which they had made suddenly moved its wings and launched itself into the air. Soon it was high above the ground, circling over the children's hut. A few minutes later it was gone, and the children knew that their brother was happy at last.

6
Bad Uncles

The Chief Kgalabetla was known by all to be a good chief. He was not one to take sides with one person against another, but would find the things on which they could all agree and chose those as the things to do. Nor would he allocate good land to one man every year and bad land to another; rather, he would share these good things amongst all the people who lived over in that place.

This chief was also very old. He had seen more things than anybody else in the village and he could remember the details of everything that had happened.

He could also remember cattle, and could tell which beasts came from which place, and who their parents were. This was a very great talent, and people who heard him talking about cattle would stand there with their mouths open in wonderment. They all said that it was remarkable good fortune to have such a wise chief in their midst.

But unfortunately, Chief Kgalabetla was extremely old. He was the oldest man in the village by far, although there were two women who were older than he was. The chief was always very kind and respectful towards these old women, as they knew a great deal too and they had seen many things happen during their lives.

When the chief called a kgotla meeting the people were very surprised. They were surprised because he had not told them the reason for the meeting beforehand, so when people arrived they were not sure what it would all be about. Some people thought that the meeting had been called to discuss when the rains might be expected to arrive, but others said that this was unlikely. So nobody really knew why the meeting was to be held.

When everybody was assembled at the kgotla, there was much excitement in the crowd. People sat on the ground or stood near the walls and talked to one another in raised voices, wondering what the chief would say. When he arrived, the women made their special calling sound to welcome the wise old man and to show how much his people loved him.

The chief began to speak to the people in his ancient, wavering voice.

"I am very old now," he said, "and my ancestors are calling me. I can hear their voices. They are saying that it is time for me to go."

At this, the people of the village let out a gasp; the sound was great, like the sound of a storm passing across the sky. Then some of the people began to wail and there were those whose faces were covered with tears. So great was the love of the people for this wise chief that they could not control their sorrow.

"Do not weep for me," said the chief. "I have lived for many years and I have done many things. Now it is time to die, because that is what we all must do. But

I wish to die a happy man, knowing that you will be in the hands of a good man. My son, Ditshabe, is a good man. I have taught him much of what I know and he can learn the rest himself. You will be well looked after under his care."

The people knew that this was true. Ditshabe was just like his father, and they had all watched with relief as he grew up, as they knew that they would be safe with a young chief like that. Now that the chief had said this, the people made an effort to be cheerful, and they listened carefully as the chief ordered the preparation of the ceremony and celebrations for Ditshabe's installation.

Ditshabe and his uncles were ordered to go to the cattle post and choose thirty head of cattle to bring back for the celebrations. They were not to stay out at the post, but they were to come back as soon as they could, driving the cattle ahead of them. In the meantime the rest of the young men and women were to practise their songs and get their best clothes ready for the occasion. Everybody had something to do.

It was a long way to the cattle post, and Ditshabe and the uncles were very tired when they arrived. They lost no time, though, in gathering thirty of the best cattle and starting the journey back home.

As they walked, some of the uncles talked amongst themselves and decided that it would be best to kill Ditshabe, so that one of them could be the new chief and could rule the people as he wished. That uncle would look after the other uncles, and they would all be happier than if their nephew were to be the new chief. Halfway through the journey back, the uncles fell upon Ditshabe and struck him with some rocks that they had picked up in the bush. The young man was not expecting this attack. He fell to the ground, his bright blood gushing out on to the dry earth, like a small, red river. The uncles dug a hole and buried him, in a place where there were thorn trees. There was nobody to cry for him; only the sky and the clouds and the trees were the witnesses of this sad event.

As they continued with their journey home, the uncles planned what they would tell the chief and his people when they returned. They would say that Ditshabe had walked off the path to look for something to eat and had not come back. They would say that they had heard a roaring sound, like the sound of a hungry lion, and that he must have been eaten up by this lion, as can sometimes happen.

Shortly after they had planned this story, a brightly coloured bird landed on a tree in front of them. At first they did not see it, but when it began to sing they saw where it was sitting on a branch nearby.

"Tswiidiii phara tswiidiii phara," sang the bird. "Can you kill him just like that? I am going to tell that you have killed Chief Ditshabe."

The uncles laughed at this bird and told it to go away. Then they continued their journey and were soon back at the village, where they broke the sad news of Ditshabe's having been eaten. There was much crying in the village, and people thought it sad that at the end of such a good life the chief should be greeted with such news about his fine son.

One old woman was very sad. She sat under a tree throughout the following day, thinking about this sad event, when she suddenly heard a bird in the branches above her. She looked up and saw a brightly coloured bird, which sang to her the exact same song that it had sung to the uncles. The old woman listened carefully and went off to tell the chief what the bird had said to her.

The chief was very angry. He ordered a regiment of young men to go to the place that the bird had mentioned. There they found the body of Ditshabe. They carried him back to the chief, tears streaming down their cheeks. Everybody could tell that he had been hit with rocks and not eaten by a lion as the lying uncles had claimed.

The chief called the people together. Even after the death of his son, with the body lying there before him, the body of the boy he had loved so much, he spoke with dignity and firmness. The uncles all started to point fingers at one another, this one blaming that one, and that one blaming this one. The chief silenced them, and asked the people what should be done with the uncles.

The people said that the uncles should be killed. And so this happened.

7
Why Elephant And Hyena Live Far From People

An inquisitive boy once asked his grandmother why elephants and hyenas lived so far away from people. He thought that this might be because the elephant was so large, and needed great empty places in which to roam. As for the hyena, the boy thought that he might live far away from people because he was an animal who liked to wander at night and needed quiet paths for his wandering.

The grandmother listened to what the boy said and shook her head. She knew the answer to his questions, which she had been told many years before. Now she told the boy.

There was a great chief once. He had many fields and there were lots of people who lived on his lands. After the rains had come and made the ground wet, the people would prepare their oxen for ploughing. Then they would cut into the soft ground and the children would put in lines of seeds. More rains would come and the seeds would grow into tall plants with heavy ears of corn.

There were people who lived near a river in that chief's lands. They planted their fields carefully and all about their new plants they built fences made out of sticks and pieces of thorn tree. No cow would dare to wander into these fields and eat the plants, as the thorns at the edge would tear into her skin. For this reason the plants grew tall and the people would all think of the delicious corn that would soon be cooking in their pots.

One morning one of the boys who looked after the plants saw that a great hole had been torn through the fence of thorns. He ran into the field and cried out as he saw the damage that had been done to the plants — where there had been rows of corn there were now only flattened stalks and scattered leaves.

This boy's father wept when he saw what had happened.

"Now we shall have no food," he said, picking up the broken stalk of the tallest plant. "We shall be hungry this year."

That afternoon they rebuilt the fence, hoping that it would stop the creature from visiting their fields that night. The next morning, though, the creature had been again, making a large hole in the fence of thorns and eating up more plants than before. Everybody in the village wept that day.

*　　*　　*

In another part of that chief's lands there were other people who also felt sad. They had a great field of pumpkins, also protected by a fence of thorns. By night some creature of great cunning had burrowed underneath the fence and eaten many pumpkins. There were still some pumpkins left, but they knew that if the creature visited them again then all their pumpkins would be gone. For those people, who ate only pumpkins, this was a terrible thing to happen.

When they heard of the misfortune of the people who lived by the river, the pumpkin people walked across to the houses by the river and held a meeting.

"We have lost almost all our corn," said the river

people. "A great creature pushed through our fence of thorns as if it were nothing."

The pumpkin people nodded and said: "That creature must be an elephant. Only an elephant could do that."

Then they told the river people what had happened to their field of pumpkins and the river people nodded their heads and said: "That must be a hyena. Only a hyena would have the cunning to dig his way under a fence of thorns."

There were some animals who heard the people talking in this way. They heard the sad voices of the men and saw the place where the tears had fallen on the ground. These animals, who had kind hearts, were saddened and they went off into the bush and told the other animals about what had happened. Even some birds heard the story and began to sing sad songs about it.

Of course it was not long before the elephant and the hyena heard what was being said about them. All the other animals now said that they were wicked and that they should not have caused so much sadness to the growers of the crops. The elephant felt ashamed when he realized

68

what the other animals were saying about him and so he went to see the hyena.

"Everybody is calling us evil," he said. "They shake their heads when they mention our names and say that there is enough food for everybody without our stealing the food of other people."

The hyena felt ashamed too and he lowered his head to the ground and howled through his yellow teeth.

"I do not like to think of my name being so bad," he said to the elephant. "Let's go to the chief and ask him to change our names."

The elephant thought that this was a good idea. Once he was no longer called an elephant, then he would be able to hold his head up again among the other animals.

"We shall set off early tomorrow morning," he said to the hyena. "It is a long way to that chief's house and we shall need all day to travel."

*   *   *

69

The next morning the two friends set off just as the first light of the sun came over the top of the hills. They walked through the bush all morning and stopped only for a short time at midday. Throughout the afternoon they walked, following the path that led to the chief's village, watching the sun go slowly down the sky. At last, just as the sun sank and the first of the stars began to glimmer above them, they saw the fires of the chief's village.

The chief's messenger welcomed them at the entrance to the village. He had heard of the bad name of the elephant and the hyena, but because they were visitors to the chief he did not show his feelings about them.

"We have come to have our names changed," explained the hyena, his red eyes glowing in the darkness.

The chief's messenger listened politely and then said: "I'm sorry, but it's too late for the chief to change your names. He can do that tomorrow morning when it

70

is light and he can see what he is doing. I shall get some boys to show you to your sleeping quarters for the night."

A tall boy came and took the elephant to the place where he was to sleep. Because he was so large, this had to be in a field. The boy wished the elephant a good night and then he took the hyena to his place. Not being so large, the hyena was able to sleep in a hut, and was given the skin of a water-buck with which to cover himself.

"At night there are only stars in the sky," said the boy. "You will need this skin to keep you warm."

The hyena thanked him and settled down in a corner of the hut and began to cover himself with the skin. The boy closed the door of the hut and went back to the chief's messenger.

"Our guests have gone to bed," he said.

"Good," said the messenger. "They can speak to the chief when the sun comes up and he can change their names then. That will make them happy."

Just before the first light of the morning, the hyena crept out of his hut and made his way to the elephant's sleeping field. He walked low down, his head dropped, as if he were sneaking away in shame — just the way that all hyenas walk. Standing in the field, waiting for his friend, the elephant also had his head lowered, his tusks almost touching the ground.

"I am very ashamed of myself," the elephant said, even before the hyena could wish him good morning. "They put me in this field of corn to sleep and during the night I ate it all."

The hyena looked at the field. It was covered with the stalks of felled plants, as if a great wind had blown upon it during the night.

"I am also ashamed," he said to the elephant. "They gave me a skin last night to cover myself and I ate it all up. Only the end of the tail is left."

The two bad friends were now too ashamed to go before the chief to ask him to change their names. Instead they ran into the bush and found places far from people where they could live. They were still called elephant and hyena and all the other animals still said bad things about these names. That is why the elephant and the hyena live far away.

8

The Wife Who Could Not Work

When Kumalo saw the beautiful girl at her father's house he knew that he would have to marry her. The girl was shy and did not look at him, but he could tell that she was beyond doubt the most beautiful girl in that part of the country.

"How many cattle would I have to give you to marry your daughter?" he asked the father.

The father looked at Kumalo and could tell that he was a rich man.

"That girl is very beautiful," he said.

"I can see that," said Kumalo. "You must be proud of her."

"The man who marries her will have to give me lots of cattle," went on the father.

"How many?" asked Kumalo. "I am sure that I will have that many."

"Fifty," said the father.

Even for Kumalo that was a very large number of cattle, but he agreed with the father that he would give them to him in return for the privilege of marrying his daughter. The father seemed pleased and called other people across to witness the bargain.

"I must warn you about something," he said after they had agreed on the day when the cattle would be delivered. "Many beautiful girls cannot work very hard. That girl is so beautiful that she cannot work at all."

Kumalo was surprised by this, but quickly promised that the girl would never have to do any work in his household.

"That is good," said the father. "She will be happy with you."

There were other women who lived at Kumalo's place. These were aunts and cousins and other relatives, and they all had large huts where they kept all their property and ate their meals at night. They were happy living with Kumalo and they were pleased when he told them that he would be getting married. They prepared a great feast for his new wife and when she arrived they all cried with joy when they saw how beautiful she was. On the first day that she spent at Kumalo's house, people came from all the nearby hills to look at the beautiful girl. Then they went back and told their families about her beauty and about how many cattle Kumalo had given her father.

Kumalo explained to everybody at his house that his new wife was too delicate to do any work.

"This beautiful girl will have to sit in the shade all day," he said. "She can watch you work, but she must do nothing herself. I have promised her father that."

So, while the other women performed the many tasks that had to be carried out around a house, the new wife sat in the doorway of one of the huts and watched them go about their tasks. She said nothing while she watched, but the women could feel her eyes on them as they worked.

After a few weeks, Kumalo's senior cousin complained to one of the other women about the new wife.

"She sits there all day," she said bitterly. "She eats her share of the food — and more — but she does nothing in return."

The other woman agreed.

"I have seen her too," she said. "There is no reason why she should not do some work as well. She has the strength."

Other women, hearing these remarks, joined in the protests. They did not say anything to Kumalo himself, knowing that he had promised his father-in-law that the new wife should not work, but every day now they stared at the new wife and tried to make her feel guilty about not working. The new wife, however, just stared back at the other women, a sweet smile on her face.

Eventually the senior cousin decided that she would act. She had had enough of watching the new wife do nothing while the rest of them laboured and she went up to her and told her that the time had come for her to work. Kumalo had gone to a far place to buy cattle and would not be back until the next day – it would be safe for them to make the new wife work.

The new wife did not object. Rising to her feet, she asked the senior cousin what she had to do and quietly took the calabash that was given to her.

"It is easy work just to fill this small calabash with water," said the cousin. "Even a beautiful woman like you can do that."

The other women stopped their work and watched the new wife walk off towards the river. As she disappeared into the thick grass that grew there, they all laughed.

"At long last that lazy woman is having to work," they said. "Today at least she cannot sit in her doorway and watch us working."

*   *   *

The new wife found the place in the river where water was to be drawn. She filled the calabash with ease and then turned round to begin her walk back. As she walked across the sandbank at the edge of the river, though, she felt the weight of the calabash getting greater and greater. She sensed the sand coming up around her ankles and found that it was more and more difficult to lift her feet. Then she found that her feet were sinking and that no matter what she did she could not free them. She was so light and delicate that the weight of the calabash was pushing her down into the ground, and in the time that it takes a bird to fly from one tree to another she had sunk completely out of sight.

The other women waited for her to return to the house so that they could laugh at her and send her back to the river for more water. After they had waited for some time, they began to feel uneasy.

"Perhaps she has run away," said one of the women.

"She would not do that," another said. "She must be hiding. She is trying to give us a fright."

The senior cousin decided that they should go and find the new wife and so the women all left their work and followed the footprints down to the river bank.

They searched and searched all along the river and in the bush beside it, but there was no trace of the new wife. Wailing loudly, they returned to the house wondering what they would be able to tell Kumalo when he came back the following day.

"We shall say that she was eaten by a lion," suggested one of the women. "That way he will not be able to blame us."

Kumalo came back to the house early the next morning bringing with him the cattle that he had bought. He was in a good mood after having bought fine cattle, but his smile faded when he saw that his new wife was not in her usual place.

"Where is my beautiful wife?" he asked the women.

"She was sitting in her doorway when I left."

The women all looked at the senior cousin, who answered with the lie that she had prepared.

"A lion ate her," she said. "We tried to stop it, but it was too hungry."

Kumalo looked at his senior cousin.

"You are lying," he said. "A lion would not choose a delicate girl like that. It would rather eat a fat woman like you."

The cousin said nothing, but when Kumalo shook his fist at her she told the truth.

"We only asked her to do a little work," she whined. "It was not too hard."

Kumalo did not listen any more. Immediately he ran to a man who lived nearby who knew all about finding people who had been lost. This man listened to Kumalo's sad story and then told him what to do.

"Go to the side of the river," he said. "Beat this small drum and get a fat woman to jump hard on the ground. That will bring back your beautiful wife."

83

Kumalo ran back to his house, the sound of his beating heart loud in his ears. He called the senior cousin to follow him and made his way quickly to the side of the river. There he played the drum, while the senior cousin jumped up and down on the sand. It was hard for her to do this, as she was so fat, but each time she showed signs of slowing down Kumalo would shout at her and urge her on.

At last they saw the sand parting and the head of the new wife slowly appeared.

"Jump faster!" ordered Kumalo, and as the senior cousin continued to jump the rest of the new wife was forced up out of the sand.

When the new wife had risen completely out of the sand, Kumalo went forward and embraced her tenderly. Then he led her back to the place where she used to sit and watch the women working. The senior cousin, ashamed of what they had done, promised they would never ask the new wife to work again. Although he was angry with the other women, Kumalo forgave them, and that night they all had a feast to celebrate the return of the new wife to her husband.

9
Bad Blood

There was a woman who lived in a village near the end of the land. This woman had two sons, one called Diepe and the other Diepetsana. They were very poor people and they did not have a great deal to eat. Their granary was never more than half full and they wore very shabby clothes. Sometimes they had no clothes at all, and had to wear old rags and leaves to preserve their modesty. It was not easy being that poor.

In the same village there was a young man called Dimo. He was not as poor as these other two, as he had married the daughter of a rich man. He had everything that he needed in this life, including a great deal of food. This food, which was rich and good, had made him quite fat.

This Dimo asked Diepe whether he could come and help him at the cattle post of his wife's parents. There was much to be done there, he said, and they would be looked after well. Because he was poor and had nothing else to do, Diepe agreed to accompany Dimo to this place, which was very far away, and on the edge of the place where nobody lived but only wild animals.

During their first evening at the cattle post, Dimo's wife brought water to the hut to wash the hands of the men before they had food. Dimo asked Diepe whose food he would be eating and said that because it belonged to the parents of his wife, it was not right that Diepe should eat it. So Diepe went to bed without any food and his stomach was empty and painful within him.

That night, Dimo went outside and killed some sheep which were in a stockade. Then he took the blood of the sheep and put it in a calabash. Back in the hut, while Diepe was fast asleep, Dimo put the sheep blood all over the sleeping man's face. The next morning, when the parents of Dimo's wife went out to look at their animals they found that the sheep had all been killed.

"Who has done this wicked thing?" they asked.

Dimo pointed at Diepe, and said, "His face is covered with sheep blood. Look! That is the person who has done this wicked thing."

The parents then said that Diepe should be killed for having done this, and that happened that afternoon. Dimo was pleased, and when he went back to the place where Diepe's brother lived, he told Diepe's mother that her son was being well looked after in that other place and that now he had come to take Diepetsana to join him. Dietpetsana was very pleased to go with Dimo, although he could tell that there was something wrong. Diepetsana was a traditional doctor and would be very good at sensing such things when he was older. But even now he could tell that there was something wicked planned, and he took with him two very important fly whisks that were good for all sorts of tasks.

They reached the cattle post and Diepetsana saw that there was no sign of his brother. That night he slept in a hut, but before he lay down he set up the fly whisks so that they would see if anybody came in at night. One was placed at the foot of his sleeping mat and another at the top.

In the depths of the night the fly whisk at the top of the sleeping mat sang out: "Who is this entering?"

And the reply came from the fly whisk at the bottom of the sleeping mat: "Isn't it Dimo?"

"What does he have on his hand?" sang the top fly whisk.

And the bottom fly whisk sang "Isn't it blood?"

Dimo was very frightened when this happened and he withdrew from the hut. A few minutes later he plucked up the courage to enter again, and the same thing happened. And so it went on until the morning, when the parents of Dimo's wife awoke to find their son-in-law outside the hut with a large gourd of sheep's blood and the sheep all dead upon the ground.

They were very angry and killed Dimo on the spot. They were pleased with Diepetsana, though, and they rewarded him handsomely. He was now a rich man and he looked after his mother well, so that she was no longer poor. Their life had changed, although they still felt sad for the loss of Diepe and thought often of their brother and son who had now gone.

10

Two Bad Friends

When an important chief died down in that far part of the country, there were many people who went to see him buried. It was a time of great sorrow, as this chief had ruled over many people for many years and had been the son of one who had served with a very great chief.

Two friends, who liked to play tricks on one another and on other people, decided that they would go to the burial too. They walked past a place where there were many mourners, all sitting under a tree and singing about how sad they were that the chief had died.

"We are very sad too," the two friends said. "We

are sad because that great chief was our father."

When they heard this, the people under the tree were surprised. They asked the two friends if they were sure that the chief was their father, and they replied that they were.

"You must give us money," one friend said. "You must give us money because we are the sons of the one who has died."

The people knew that they should do this, but they were unwilling to give money to people whom they did not know.

"If you come with us to the grave," they said, "then we shall be able to find out whether you really are the sons of that great chief."

The two friends agreed to do this. There was no reason for them to refuse to go to the grave, and already they were thinking of ways of fooling these people under the tree.

When they reached the grave, there were many people milling about, calling out in sorrow and saying how sad they were that the chief had gone. Even those who had not liked the chief were there, saying that they were more sorry than any others. If the chief had been alive, he would have been pleased to see so many of his enemies shedding so many tears on his death.

The people from under the tree told one of the friends to stand by the side of the grave. He did this, but while he was moving into that position, the other friend hid in a bush which grew near the edge of the grave.

Then one of the people from under the tree called out into the sky.

"Is it true that these men are your sons?"

Everybody was surprised when a voice called out:

"They are my sons. And you must give them lots of money."

"The chief himself has spoken to us," the people from under the tree said. "We must do as he says."

The other friend then slipped out of the bush. The voice had been his, of course, but everybody had thought that it had come from the grave.

95

The two friends stood respectfully by the grave while people walked past and put money into a box which one of the friends had with him. Then, crying loudly to show how sad they were, they walked back to the house of one of them.

"I shall keep the money here until it is counted," said the friend whose house it was. "Then one day you may come and claim your half share."

The next day, the friend returned to the house of the friend who had kept the money. That friend's wife greeted him sadly and told him that his friend was unfortunately very ill and would have to stay in his bed for a long time.

"He will not be able to give you your money," she said. "He is too ill to do that."

"Then I shall wait," said the other friend. "I shall

wait by his bedside until he is better."

"That may not be for a few years," said the wife. "He says that he is very ill."

"I can wait that long," said the friend.

The wife could not persuade him to go away and so she had to show him into the friend's room. The ill friend was lying under a blanket, his face covered and only his toes showing at the end.

"I am here to wait," the friend said. "When you are better we shall be able to divide the money that those people gave us."

The friend in bed said nothing.

As the day wore on, it became hotter and hotter. The friend under the blanket began to feel as if he were in an oven, and then, at last, he had to throw the blanket aside to let cool air in.

"I am glad that you are better," his friend said to him. "Now we shall be able to divide the money."

Reluctantly, because he knew that there was nothing else he could do, the friend retrieved the box and gave his friend his share of the money. The friend thanked him and said how pleased he was that his friend had recovered from his illness.

"You are fortunate to get better in two hours rather than two years," he said. "Perhaps it is the good hot air that cured you so quickly."

The friend who had pretended to be ill buried his share of the money in a tin box. Unfortunately for him, the box had a hole in it and when he dug it up the following month the ants had eaten all the money. His wife told him that this is what happened to people who obtained money through tricks.

"The ants like to play tricks too," she said. "It is your own fault for being such a wicked trickster."

The other friend fell into a large hole on his way home from collecting the money. He was unable to get himself out of it and so he was very pleased when he saw some people walking by. These people were the people who had been under the tree.

"Please pull me out," the friend called. "I shall die if I am left down here."

The people from under the tree looked down on the friend and agreed to pull him out. They would only do so, though, if he gave them money. The friend asked how much money they needed and they replied that they would want all his money. In this way the friend in the hole had to give the people from under the tree not only his share of the money he had got by trickery, but also his own money, which he had been carrying with him. In this way, too, the people from under the tree got back exactly that amount which they had given at the burial of the chief. If the chief had been alive to see all this happening he would have said that this was the right outcome.

11

How A Strange Creature Took The Place Of A Girl And Then Fell Into A Hole

The daughter of the chief of some people near Kezi was one of the most beautiful girls in the whole of Matabeleland. The chief knew that there would be no difficulty in getting a good husband for her, but he did not want to leave anything to chance. Calling on a powerful witchdoctor, he asked him to provide charms that would be sure to attract a handsome man to the house.

The witchdoctor told the chief that this was not a difficult thing to do. The best way of attracting a handsome husband was to find a special tree, part of which would have been burned. From the burned part the girl should take a piece of charcoal and then rub this between her palms. If she did this, there would be no difficulty in finding the best possible husband.

The chief was pleased with this advice. He ordered his men to prepare food and water for a journey and then he set off with his daughter in the direction indicated by the witchdoctor.

It was harder than he had imagined to find the special tree but eventually they came to a valley where the conditions seemed right for the growth of such a tree. The chief climbed up to the top of a small hill at the entrance to this valley and looked down onto the place where he thought the tree might grow. When he saw it was there, he called out to his daughter and together they walked to the foot of the half-burned, half-green tree. Climbing up into the branches of the burned part, the chief broke off a piece of charcoal and brought it down to his daughter. She rubbed the charcoal between her palms and as she did so she described the sort of husband for whom she longed.

The girl's mother was waiting for them when they arrived home.

"A very handsome young man has arrived," she told them eagerly. "He said that he had lost his way and needed to be given directions to get to the Limpopo River."

"It is my husband!" the girl shouted out gleefully. "Please show him to me immediately!"

They took the girl to where the young man was sitting on a small rock and showed him to her. She was very pleased to see how handsome and strong he was and the father lost no time in telling the young man that he should marry his daughter. The young man said that he was happy to do this, but that he had no house of his own.

"That does not matter," said the chief. "I shall give you some poles and some thatch and you can go and build it."

The young man asked whether it would be possible for him to build his house near the house of his own father, who lived by the Limpopo River. This was some distance away, but the chief agreed that this would be quite all right, as the father of the young man was a well-known chief in that part and he would be able to protect the girl from some of the dangers that were in the Limpopo River and nearby.

The chief spent a day discussing the house and the

marriage with the young man and then sent him on his way.

"Begin the building of the house," he said to him. "In a month I shall send my daughter down to join you at your father's house. Then you can get married."

It was difficult for the girl to pass the time without thinking constantly of the husband who awaited her. Toward the end of the month, her mother became ill, and she spent much of her time at her bedside, nursing her and encouraging her to get better. The old woman, however, became weaker and weaker, although she was still able to tell her daughter how happy she was that she would soon be joining her new husband. At last the month had passed and the daughter was told that she could prepare herself for the journey. The chief fetched an ox for her to ride upon, and then he stood at the gate to bid her farewell. As she rode past him, he gave her a small flower.

"Watch this flower," he said to her. "If the flower wilts, then you will know that your mother has died."

The girl began her journey, wondering if she would ever see her mother again. By midday, she was halfway there and paused to shelter for a while under the shade of a thorn tree. It was while she sat there that the flower, which she had been grasping in her hand, suddenly withered. At this, the girl knew that her mother had died and she began to weep.

It was important to that girl that her tears should not touch the ground. As the daughter of a chief, this would have been wrong, and so she quickly sought a place where she could weep in safety. Near the thorn tree was a deep ant-hole, and the girl sat next to this, allowing her tears to disappear into the dark depths of the earth. Unknown to her, a strange animal lived in that hole, and he soon felt the warm tears falling upon his skin.

At first the girl was frightened when the strange animal came out of the hole, but when he spoke to her and reassured her she was no longer afraid. He asked her where she was going and why she was going there, and when she explained to him he quickly suggested that it would be better if he accompanied her on her journey. The girl was pleased to have company, and so she agreed that the strange animal could come with her, at least as far as the hills near her future father-in-law's house.

While the girl rode comfortably on the ox, the strange animal loped along beside her.

"Your clothes are very beautiful," he said to her. "I wish that I had clothes like that."

The girl felt sorry for the strange-looking animal and offered to allow him to try on her clothes for a short period. He was very pleased with this offer and was soon dressed in the girl's clothes, smiling to himself in his satisfaction. After they had covered a short distance, he looked up at the girl and asked her if she was comfortable on the ox.

"It is very comfortable," the girl

said. "It is much easier than walking."

The strange animal looked sad.

"I have never ridden an ox," he said. "I shall never know what it is like."

Hearing this remark, the girl leapt off the ox and told the strange animal that he should take her place.

"This is very kind of you," said the strange animal, smiling as he climbed onto the back of the ox. From where he sat, he could see the cattle pens of the father-in-law's village and he knew that they would soon be there.

The father-in-law was at the outer fence, ready to meet his new daughter-in-law. As the ox stopped in front of the village, the father-in-law stepped forward to help the strange animal get off the ox. He frowned as he did so, wondering to himself why his son had said that his new bride was so beautiful when in reality she was so ugly. Perhaps she will seem more beautiful tomorrow, he said to himself.

The real girl tried to tell her father-in-law that the strange animal was only a strange animal dressed in her clothes, but he refused to listen to her, thinking that she was only a servant girl. Telling her to keep quiet, he took the two of them to a hut he had prepared and there they were told to sleep.

The girl soon cried herself to sleep, but the strange animal nosed about the hut looking for things to eat. When he came across the calabashes of sour milk which the family kept in that hut, he drank them greedily, making a loud noise as he did so.

The next morning the family was surprised to find that their sour milk had all disappeared, but everybody thought that the calabashes must have leaked. New calabashes were obtained and these were filled with sour milk and put in the same place as the old ones. That night the strange animal again nosed about the dark corners of the hut and drank all the sour milk, turning the calabashes upside down to empty out the last drop.

The father was suspicious when he found that all the sour milk had once again disappeared and so he called everybody into the meeting area in front of his hut and told them of a plan he had.

"We have a sour milk thief among us," he said gravely. "There is only one way to find out who it is."

In the middle of the village a deep hole was dug. Into the hole four calabashes of sour milk were placed and then everybody was ordered to stand in a line. One by one, the people of the village and the visitors too were forced to jump over the hole. Most landed safely on the other side and were told to stand to one side.

When it came to the turn of the strange animal to jump, he had almost reached the other side before he tumbled down into the hole. When the people looked down to see what was happening, they saw the strange animal drinking greedily. The temptation of the sour milk had clearly been too much for him, and he had given himself away.

The father-in-law lost no time in ordering the hole to be filled in, burying the strange animal from sight. When this had been done, he turned to the girl and asked her to tell him what had happened. She told him how the strange animal had supplanted her and how nobody had been prepared to listen to her explanation at the beginning. The father-in-law realized that what she said was true and made it up to her by giving her many presents. When this happened, the girl almost entirely forgot about the strange animal and all the unhappiness which it had caused her.

12
Head Tree

A man who had never done any wrong to anybody else had a great misfortune happen to him. His wife noticed that a tree was beginning to grow out of his head. This was not painful to the man, but it made him feel awkward when there were other people about. They would point at him and say that this was a very strange thing to happen. Some people walked some miles to see this man sitting outside his hut with a tree growing out of his head.

At last the man decided that it was time to do something about the tree. He asked his wife if she would chop it down, but she warned him that this could be dangerous.

"If this tree is growing out of your head," she said, "then you might bleed to death if I chop it down."

The man agreed that this was a danger. So instead of chopping the tree down he went to see a certain woman who was well known in that part for being a woman who could use charms to solve difficult problems. This woman lived in a hut some distance away and so the man had to bear the stares of all the people as he walked to her place.

The charm woman looked at the man and said that she had never seen this sort of thing before, but that her mother had told her that things like this could happen and had given her instructions as to how to deal with it.

"You must have done something bad to have this happen to you," she said.

"I have not done anything bad," said the man hotly. "I have always behaved well."

"In that case," said the charm woman, "you must have been planning to do something bad. If this were not so, then why would a tree grow out of your head?"

The man had no answer for this, and so the charm woman took a special herb out of her bag and gave it to him.

"You must eat this every day for a week," she said. "At the end of the week the tree will go. You must also pay me two cows, for this is a very expensive herb and it is not easy to stop trees growing out of people's heads."

The man promised that he would give the woman

her cows once the tree had gone. Then he returned to his home and took the first part of the herb. At the end of the week, when he had taken the last part of the herb, the tree fell off his head. The man's wife chopped it up and they used the wood for their cooking fire. The man was very relieved, and he was now able to walk about without people pointing at him and clicking their tongues in amazement.

"You must give that woman her cows," his wife said. "She has cured you well."

"I shall not," said the man. "She is just an old witch with a sharp tongue. There is no reason to give her anything."

The charm woman heard that the tree had fallen off the man's head and she sent a young boy to tell him to send her two cows. The man listened to the message which the boy brought, but all he did was beat the boy with a stick and send him home.

The next day, when the man was sitting in front of his hut drinking his beer, his wife came to him and looked at the top of his head.

"Another tree seems to be growing," she said. "This time it looks very big."

The man's heart filled with despair. He could not face the thought of having a tree on his head again, and so he went back to the charm woman's house.

"I have come for more medicine," he said. "And I have brought those two cows I promised you."

The charm woman looked at him and shook her head.

"You are a wicked man who does not keep his promises," she said. "If you want me to cure you again and to stop that tree forever, you will have to pay me four cows."

The man stamped his feet on the ground, but he knew that she was the only woman who could stop a tree from growing out of his head. Reluctantly he brought four cows and left them in front of her house. She gave him the herb and told him that he should always keep his promises, even if he thought that he had made a promise to a weak old woman. The man said nothing, but he knew that what she said was quite right.

13

The Grandmother Who Was Kind To A Smelly Girl

A beautiful girl had a very handsome makgabe, which is the apron worn by very young girls. This had been made for her by her grandmother, who was very kind to her. The grandmother had spent many hours weaving this makgabe for the girl.

The other girls in that place were jealous of that makgabe. Their own aprons were fine, but not so fine as the apron that that girl wore. They looked at her makgabe and thought that it would be better for them if they could get rid of it. But how do you take a person's clothes when that person is wearing them? That is a very difficult thing, even for clever girls.

One morning the girls invited that girl to go swimming with them in a river nearby. When they arrived at the river bank, the other girls said that they would all need to take off their makgabes, as the cloth would be damaged if it got wet. So all the girls did this, including the girl with the very beautiful makgabe.

When they were all naked, they jumped into the water and splashed around for some time. Then they emerged and the leader of the jealous girls took the makgabe of that girl and threw it into the river, near a place where a very large snake lived on the river bank. Then all the other girls put on their makgabes and walked home, leaving that girl crying by the river, saddened by the loss of her beautiful apron.

124

The large snake heard her weeping and came out to see what was happening. When he saw this beautiful girl, he slithered out and swallowed the makgabe and the girl. Fortunately for her, the snake did not like the taste of the makgabe, and he spat both it and the girl out, leaving them lying on the bank covered with the slime which is to be found in a snake's stomach. This slime smells very bad.

The girl put on her fouled makgabe and ran home to her parents, singing:

> Mother, open the door for me, I am smelling;
> Mother, open the door for me, I am smelling,
> I am smelling very bad.

The mother heard this song and ran out of their house to sing back to the girl before she could come in:

> Go away, you are smelling,
> Go away, you are smelling,
> Go away, you are smelling very bad.

*   *   *

The girl was very upset by this, and ran off to the house of her aunt and uncle. They heard her singing her song as she approached. They ran out, as had her mother, and sang the same song that her mother had sung, telling her to go away because she smelled so bad.

The poor girl then had only her grandmother's house to go to. She set off in that direction, her heart heavy within her. It seemed as if nobody wanted to look after her now that she smelled so bad. But she was wrong. When she reached her grandmother's house, the old woman did not send her away, but took her in and washed her, and her makgabe, making everything smell sweetly. Then the girl stayed there and some years later she received a proposal of marriage from the son of a very rich chief. The parents heard about this and asked her to come back to their house and live there.

The girl, however, remembered how they had behaved when she had smelled so bad, and so she told them that she would never go back to their house, even if they were her parents.

"Parents must love their children," she said, "even if their children smell very bad."

After her marriage, the girl invited the grandmother to come and live with her in the house of this rich chief and his son. The grandmother was happy to do this, and she was very comfortable there, and very important.

14

The Baboons Who Went This Way And That

There was much unhappiness in a village of small huts. The people who lived there had been happy before, but then wild animals had come and had begun to frighten them. These animals ate all their crops and from time to time they even carried off children who wandered away from their parents. It was not a good place to live any longer, and the people began to think of where they might go to lead a new life.

One family found the answer. Rather than deal with the wild animals who seemed to be everywhere on the flat land, they decided to go in search of food up in the hills. It was not hard to find food there. There were bushes that grew in the cracks between rocks; there were trees that grew at the foot of the slopes; there were rock rabbits which could be trapped and birds which could be brought down with the stones which littered the floor of the caves.

Other families noticed how well the hill family was doing. They saw the sleekness of their children, and they noticed how calm the parents were.

"It is a good life that we lead up in the hills," said the husband. "You should come there too."

Soon the other families abandoned their homes on the flat land and went up to the hills. Each family found a cave to live in, and in this way they were warm and secure. Soon everybody talked about how sorry they were that they had not come to the hills earlier, rather than letting the wild animals eat their crops and drag off their children.

As the children grew up in the hills, they began to get better at the things that had to be done to live in such a place. They became very quick at climbing rocks, and even the youngest could scamper up a face of rock almost as quickly as any rock rabbit. They also became good at climbing into trees to look for fruit, and they could swing in the branches almost as well as any monkey. People who passed by and saw the hill people living on their hill wondered whether they were perhaps wild animals, but when they saw their faces and the clothes that they were wearing they realized that they were only people who had made the hills their home.

Slowly, things began to change. The parents noticed that their children were talking less, and that rather than speaking to one another in the language of people they were beginning to use grunts. Then the adults themselves noticed that their noses were getting bigger and that they were growing hairier. Every time they looked at one another they saw that their faces had changed yet more and that their teeth were longer. Soon they spent as much time on four legs as on two, and it was at this point that they became a new creature. This creature, which had never before been seen in that place, was the creature which people now call the baboon.

For a time, the baboons lived happily. They stopped chasing the rock rabbits and started to eat grubs from the ground. They also forgot how to talk, and nobody now made any sound other than a bark or a grunt. They took off their clothes and let the rags lie on the ground until they were destroyed by ants. Their legs and arms were now completely covered with dark hair.

They still remembered, though, that they had been people, and this was something which made them worried. When they looked into each other's faces, they realized that their noses were now much bigger than they had been before, and this made them jeer. Every baboon laughed at every other baboon, pointing at his enlarged nose and throwing his hands about in mirth. This made the baboon who was being laughed at angry. He would jump up and down in anger, all the while laughing at the large nose of the other.

Eventually the mockery became so great that the baboons could no longer bear to be together. Each family split off and lived by itself, laughing at the others because of their great noses, but not liking to be laughed at for their own noses. That is why baboons live in small groups today and do not live as a baboon nation, as do men and many other animals.

15
The Thathana Moratho Tree

A certain man liked trees. He had many trees in the ground behind his house, and he was very proud of these. There were trees for all purposes – a tree to attract birds that might sing well; a tree that had good branches for making fires; a tree that would keep away snakes because they were frightened of it. There were many trees, and the people in that place would come and look at them from time to time and wish that they had trees like his.

There was one tree that this man had planted which nobody else had in their yard. This was the thathana moratho tree, and he had given very strict instructions that nobody at all, not even his children, should ever touch this tree. Nobody knew why they were not allowed to touch this tree, but since the tree belonged to this man they accepted the rule. They could look at it, though, and many people did this, wondering what was so special about this particular tree.

This man had a child called Ntshetsanyana, who was looked after by a servant girl. One morning the child was very hungry and cried and cried for food. The servant looked for food with which to feed her charge, but found none. Eventually she went out into the yard, picked some of the fruit from the thathana moratho tree and gave it to the child.

The child said, "What is this very good fruit?"

The servant girl replied, "It is the fruit of the thathana moratho tree and you can eat it. I am telling you to eat it. I have picked it for you because you are so hungry and have been crying so much. Now you must eat it."

The child took the fruit from the servant girl and ate it. It was very good, and the child smiled happily after the last morsel had been consumed. It was the best fruit that had ever been brought into the house, and the child hoped that there would be more chances to eat this fruit in the future.

When the man came back to his house he discovered what had happened and he was very angry. He shouted at the servant girl, who wept and cringed. The man told her that by feeding his child fruit from the thathana moratho tree, she had insulted him. Now he would have to take her to Chief Mmeke, who was a very stern chief. He knew the chief would kill both the girl and the child for doing this prohibited thing.

They set off together, with the servant girl carrying the child and the man driving them on, muttering to himself about the great insult that had been done him by this act of disobedience. On their way, they met a friend of this man, who asked them what was happening. The man explained about the insult, but the poor girl replied with a song:

> He is lying: I did not insult him.
> I only took thathana moratho;
> I gave it to Ntshetsanyana
> Who was crying.
> Now I am to be taken to Mmeke,
> Mmeke the ruthless one.

The man, however, did not wish to listen to her and he pushed her with a stick, making her continue her journey to the place of Chief Mmeke, where she would be killed.

Some time later, while still walking under the burning sun, they met the son of Chief Mmeke. He asked what was happening and the girl immediately sang him the same song. This time, the song was believed and the chief's son, a kind young man, fell in love with the girl. He said that he would go with them to the chief's place, although he did not say what he was planning to do once they got there.

"Do not kill this girl, Father," said the young man. "She is very beautiful and I wish to marry her."

The chief listened to this, and then he listened to the man who had brought the girl to be killed. After the man had finished speaking, the chief said, "Go home now, and leave this bad girl here. She will be killed tonight, when it is dark."

The man was satisfied with this and he went away. They did not kill the girl, though: the chief's son married her and she became a very good wife for him. They had many fine sons, and she was very popular with Chief Mmeke himself, who was pleased that he had been kind to this girl.

16

Chicken, Hawk And The Missing Needle

It might be hard to believe this, but Chicken and Hawk used to be very good friends. They could be seen sitting on the ground, telling one another stories, and sharing food. And if anybody was rude to Chicken, or called her names, Hawk would soon make him apologize to her friend. And if Hawk was ever too tired to hunt, Chicken would carry food to her from her own food store and place it at her feet. It was a very good friendship.

Chicken was good at sewing, but because she was poor she only had one needle. With this needle she sewed clothes for her family, including a fine red jacket for her husband. She also made clothes for other people, who paid her to do this, although they could not give her very much. She used this money to buy food for her chicks, who were always hungry, as they were growing up and needed to eat to keep up their strength.

Then Chicken lost her needle. It was there one moment and then it was not. She looked about her and saw that there was a great deal of dust there, and sand, and other things that will swallow a needle. Now she was very sad. Without that needle she could not sew any clothes, and that meant that she would not have money to buy food for her family.

'What are we to do?' asked one of her children. 'Now that you have lost the needle, we shall all starve. It is very sad.'

Hawk heard of the loss of her friend's needle. She came to see her and said, 'I have a needle, and I shall be happy to lend it to you. I do not like to see my friend so sad.'

Chicken was very relieved. 'You are a very good friend,' she said. 'Now I shall be able to earn money for my family. I am lucky to have a friend like you.'

Hawk brought the needle to Chicken and she started to sew again. She sewed a new pair of trousers for her husband and some clothes which she sold by the side of the road to people who passed by. She was very happy.

But then she discovered one morning that the needle was not in its usual place. She started to search for it, but could not find it anywhere. And that morning, when Hawk came to see her and asked where the needle was, Chicken had to admit that she had lost it.

Hawk said: 'I lent you that needle on the condition that you would give it back to me when I had to do my own sewing. If you do not find it, I shall punish you by eating your chicks.' And with that cruel threat, Hawk flew off, leaving her friend in a state of panic, running around and scratching here and there and everywhere in the dusty soil, looking for the lost needle.

She could not find it. She scratched and scratched in the soil with her claws, sending up little clouds of dust, but all to no avail. She knew now that her children were not safe, as Hawk flew high in the sky, circling over the land, and her shadow was like a moving black hand of of death. When Chicken saw this shadow she would run to muster her children and take them to shelter. And when she drank, Chicken would take the water in her mouth quickly and look up into the sky to see if Hawk was coming.

In this way two old friends have ceased to be friends to one another. Chicken still scratches in the ground, looking for Hawk's needle, and Hawk still circles in the sky looking for Chicken's children on the ground below. It will be like this until the needle is found, which many people doubt will ever happen, as a needle is a small thing. But for Hawk, and Chicken, it is a big thing – big enough to end a friendship for ever.

17
Morategi And His Two Wives

Morategi was a rich man who had two of everything, including two wives. There was no shortage of food in his household, as he had good fields and many cattle. His children were fat and their skin was shiny from all the good food that they ate. And his wives were happy. They both loved their husband and they were also very fond of one another. They never fought over anything.

Everybody was very happy in that household until a bad drought came to the land. Where once good tall grass had grown, now there was none. The cattle grew bony as there was less and less for them to eat and the people grew thinner too, just like the cattle. Then the cattle died, and when that happened the man, his two wives and the children cried and cried for what they had lost.

Morategi decided that the only thing for him to do was to go to a nearby village and take a job. So he left, taking the senior wife with him. He soon found a job which, although it was hard work, provided him with food. He bought sorghum, maize and beans. His wife, who also worked in that place, bought pumpkin seeds.

When they had enough food, they returned to their place and shared the food with the other wife and with all the children. Everybody was pleased now, as they had enough to eat and were no longer hungry.

But food does not last forever, and soon it was necessary for Morategi to go off to work again. This time he took the junior wife. Again they worked very hard and made enough money to buy food for the whole family. The junior wife used the money she had earned to buy a large pot, which she took home with her.

The senior wife was very impressed with this pot and congratulated the junior wife for all her hard work and the rewards that it had brought. The pot, which was very pretty to look at, was put in a hut at the back, as it was too good to be used for everyday purposes and would be kept for special occasions. This place where it was kept was also the place where seeds were stored, and some of these were pumpkin seeds.

One afternoon the junior wife decided that she would use the pot to cook a special meal for the family. She went into the hut to fetch her pot and discovered to her surprise that a pumpkin seed had taken root in the pot and had grown into a fine yellow pumpkin. But she was not pleased with this and went to the senior wife and shouted at her that she should remove her pumpkin. The senior wife went to look at the pumpkin. She liked it very much and said that she was unwilling to cut it up and remove it from the pot.

The two wives were very angry with one another. They argued and shouted at one another and gave Morategi no peace. If anybody had visited that house during that time they would have been very surprised to hear that this was the house in which people used to get on so well with one another.

Eventually Morategi could stand it no longer and he made a plan to stop this constant arguing about pots and pumpkins. He went to see a very wise traditional doctor and asked him to tell the wives that their husband had become very ill and that the only way in

which his life might be saved was if they fed him immediately with a fine yellow pumpkin.

When they received this message, the two women
rushed to the hut where the pot was stored. Picking up
two sharp stones which were lying about in that place,
they smashed the pot and took out the pumpkin, which
they cooked for their husband. Now there was nothing
left to argue about, and they started to be polite to one
another again.

The husband ate the pumpkin, which tasted very
good. Then he told the wives about his trick, and they
all laughed. Happiness had returned to that household
at long last, and all that it had cost was a pot.

18
The Miracle Tree

There were children who lived in a small village by a river. Nothing very much happened in that village, and there was hardly ever any water in the river. But there was a special tree just outside the village, and this tree was unlike any other tree in the whole country. It was a miracle tree, and the people were very proud of it.

'This may be a small village,' they said. 'But at least we have the miracle tree.'

Then there came a big storm. The country had been parched and dry, with the land crying out for water, but now even the normally empty river in that village was a raging torrent. And in the sky there were heavy clouds, high and purple, and lightning that joined the sky to the land with great flashes and bangs.

One of these bolts of lightning hit the miracle tree. When this happened, some of the branches on the tree burned up and the leaves on the tree all shrivelled. Afterwards, when the storm had passed, the land turned green with new grass. But the miracle tree remained black and shrivelled. It had no new leaves and it gave no fruit.

The people were very sad about what had happened to their tree and many of the children cried because they missed the fruit that the tree had so generously given them. Nobody went near the tree for a long time, but then one day a child went there and she ran straight home after she had looked at the tree.

'There is a woman living in the tree,' she said to her mother. 'She has only one eye in the middle of her head, like the light of a train.'

The mother laughed at this child, and said that it was impossible that a woman should be living in the tree and also impossible that she should have only one eye in the middle of her head. But secretly the mother went to visit the tree and she saw that what the child had said was true. There was indeed a one-eyed woman living on top of the tree.

For a long time nobody went near the tree, as they were all afraid of the strange woman who lived on top of it. But then the same child who had first seen the woman went back and she saw that the woman had died and that there was nobody living on the tree.

Not long after that, after word had got out that the woman who lived in the tree had died, a family went to the tree and started to pick the fruit that was growing on it. To their surprise, the tree began to shake and then changed into a lion. They were very afraid, especially when the lion began to sing. The words of the song warned people not to try to pick the fruit of the tree.

As they ran away, the people looked back and saw that the tree had changed again. Now it was a river!

'This is really a miracle tree,' said a small boy who

had seen this. 'First it was a lion and then it was a river. Perhaps it will be something else now.'

He was right. When they looked back next, they saw that the tree had become a tree again.

Many days later, another family passed by the tree and, seeing the fruit that it bore, started to pick some of it. This made the tree shake.

'Look,' shouted one of the children of this family.

'There is a crocodile up in the tree.'

The family ran away when they saw the head of the crocodile peering down at them. They did not go back to the tree again, and nor did anybody else. And from that time onwards, nobody in that village spoke about the miracle tree. They thought that it was better to be a quiet village where nothing happened, rather than a village where too much happened.

19
The Goat
And The Jackal

Goat and Jackal were very good friends. They were always to be seen eating together and telling one another stories. Goat would tell a story and jackal would howl with laughter. Then Jackal would reply with his own story and Goat would make a very strange sound that showed that he, too, thought this was very funny.

When Goat invited Jackal one day to come and have dinner with him, Jackal was very pleased. Goat had said that he would have some very fine meat for them to eat, and Jackal liked to eat fine meat.

Goat was a good cook.

'This meat is very tasty,' said Jackal, as he sat at Goat's table, the plate of meat before him. 'Is it the meat of a guinea fowl?'

'No,' said Goat. 'It is the meat of a rooster.'

'Then you must get me the chicks of this rooster so that I can eat them too,' said Jackal.

Goat laughed at this, and explained to Jackal that a rooster was a man and could not have chicks. Only women can have babies, he said.

Jackal was very cross at being corrected and told Goat that unless she fetched the chicks of this rooster he would have to eat him instead. This made Goat very frightened, as jackal had powerful jaws and could easily eat him up if he wanted to. He tried again to explain to Jackal that a rooster could not have chicks, but his friend just became angrier and angrier and started to snarl at him, as if he was preparing to eat him.

Then Hare came to Goat's house and saw the danger that his friend was facing. Without delay he turned to Jackal and said that he could not stay to talk to him as he had to go to go and cook for his father, who had a small baby.

Jackal turned to him angrily and said it was strange that he should say this as his father was a man and men did not have babies. 'You must be strange in the head to say such a thing,' said Jackal.

Hare looked at Goat and gave him a wink. Jackal did not see this wink.

'But you said exactly the same thing,' he pointed out.

'You said that a rooster could have chicks. You must be strange in the head too.'

When Jackal heard this he was so embarrassed that he ran away. Goat turned to Hare and thanked him for saving his life. Then they both sat down and ate the last of the meat, which was very good.